CURSED IN STONE

Book One By

LIA DAVIS

Sunstone's Fire
Cursed in Stone, book 1
By: Lia Davis

Published by After Glows
© 2015 Lia Davis

eBook ISBN: 978-1-944060-06-0
Print ISBN: 978-1-944060-07-7

Cover Art by Fiona Jayde Media

All characters in this book are fiction and figments of the author's imagination.

**www.AuthorLiaDavis.com
AfterGlowsPublishing.com**

Dedication

To my amazing friend and sister in everything that matters, Kerry Adrienne. Thank you for taking this journey with me.

Sunstone's Fire

Aspiring author, Nate Wilson wants some space from his overbearing family and a job he doesn't like. A week on the Oregon coast sounds like paradise and just what he needs to get the creative juices flowing. Unfortunately, his plans are derailed when a storm moves in and a ghostly figure flashes in his headlights, sending him skidding off the road and into a tree. Lucky for him, he ends up in front of a Bed and Breakfast, and the beautiful owner may do more to spur his creativity than any beach could.

Hesitant witch and inn owner, Haylee Clark is cursed. Well, not her exactly—at least not yet—but all of the women in her family have suffered the same fate. They fell in love, only to have that passion turn sour and their husbands die tragically, leaving them brokenhearted. So far, Haylee has done well to avoid that destiny, but when the captivating Nate Wilson crashes into her life, he awakens something within her that she never thought to feel.

When the pair stumbles upon a hidden room where Haylee's grandmother used to conduct her rituals, they unknowingly unleash a dark entity hell-bent on destruction, and discover that a family heirloom is the source of the Clark family curse. Despite the spell, they can't deny their attraction, and give in to the magic between them. But the closer Haylee and Nate get, the more the curse tries to tear them apart. If they don't find a way to defeat the evil, they may lose more than their hearts.

Prologue

Lafayette, Oregon

Wind whipped through the trees and blew fallen leaves across the cemetery, bringing the scents of rain. Constantine's bones ached, and he had an itch he couldn't scratch. The longing to be free, to stretch his tired, stiff muscles didn't help matters. He was stuck. Forever frozen in stone, except for three nights a month. For now, all he could do was watch dark clouds move in, covering the setting sun.

Lifting his gaze, he stared at the large, three-story house across the road. A Bed and Breakfast, from the sign out front. The large, grey stone building loomed over the street and its dark shadow stretched to him, stopping a few feet from where he perched on a headstone. Ivy crawled up both sides of the house in an eerily possessive way, like it was protecting those within from the spirits outside.

And there were many. He could feel the ghosts lurking in the darker corners of the cemetery, waiting, growing restless. Very much like he was.

Soon. The rise of the full moon was a couple of hours away. Then he'd be free for the next three days to search for the book and a link to his past and his lost love.

Sorrow seeped into his heart once more. His chest ached and a tear rolled down his stone cheek. Amara — his love — was long gone, for too much time had passed since he'd been cursed for loving her.

A fatal kiss, forbidden love – cursed in stone.
Guard from above to watch others love.

It was his curse. At least, the first few lines of the incantation. That was all he could remember. Everything else was a faded memory. Yet, he didn't fully understand what it meant. *To watch others love.* As in others' happiness while he remained a gargoyle, unable to move or sleep? At least not until the three days of the full moon's light, where he was finally able to walk as a man.

Suddenly, he jerked his gaze back to the house. A light flicked on in one of the top-floor windows. A dark, inky power pulled at his subconscious, calling to him. The familiar energy seemed to grow stronger by the moment.

Odd. He'd never been drawn to a place before. Sure, he was flashed from one city to another right before the full moon, but never to a specific building. Not like the pull he felt with the Bed and Breakfast in front of him. Could the book he sought be in there?

There was only one way to find out. Once he was able to move, he would investigate the power radiating from the inn.

Just then, a brown leather wallet materialized in mid-air then dropped to the ground. A moment later, a female's voice whispered on the wind. *"Find the stone."*

Chapter One

Lightning cracked across the dark, cloud-covered sky, illuminating the street. Great. Just what he needed. A storm. On his vacation. Although the rain would match his mood.

Nate gripped the wheel a little tighter. He shouldn't be as annoyed as much as he was, but lately, it seemed he couldn't catch a break. He was single, his family was always in his business, and his job sucked. He'd hit a crossroads in his life. His career, if he wanted to call it that, wasn't what he wanted to do with the rest of his life. Even though Wilson Enterprises was the family business and he was expected to follow in his father's and brothers' footsteps. He didn't want to be stuck in an office all day. He longed to travel, see the world.

At thirty-five, it was time to start looking to where he wanted to be five or ten years from now. The vacation was a way to get out of town, change the scenery, and a means to clear his head. The destination wasn't important. Neither was the weather.

It could rain all it wanted.

Another flash of lightning lit up the night. A woman dressed in a long, white gown with hair the color of night appeared in the middle of the road. Fear and panic burned his gut as he jerked the steering wheel to avoid hitting her. The car swerved. Out of reflex, he hit the brakes, causing the vehicle to spiral out of control onto the shoulder, ending by crashing into a large tree. His forehead slammed into the steering wheel. Pain arched through his skull and he groaned. Lifting his head, he scanned the area for the woman, but she wasn't there. Had he imagined the whole thing?

After a few moments, a tap on the window jerked his attention to a dark-hooded figure standing outside the driver's side door. Or was it minutes? The fact that he hadn't noticed her there worried him that he might have lost consciousness.

When he glanced back out the windshield, he noted the fat raindrops pounding on the glass. Frowning, he took his keys from the ignition and opened the door. Big, blue eyes glanced up at him from under the hood of a coat then blinked. A woman, but not the one that had caused him to crash. This woman's sensual, full lips frowned as she asked, "Are you all right?"

He nodded. The pain in his head eased slightly. "Yeah."

"Come out of the rain." She wrapped her black rain jacket tighter around her and darted up a stone pathway to a large, dark old house covered in ivy.

After a quick glance up and down the street and at the cemetery across from them, Nate looked at his car and shook his head. It hissed from having the front smashed. He wasn't one to become attached to things, yet he'd had the car since college. And this was the first accident he'd had. Letting out a sigh, he threaded a hand through his wet hair and followed the woman up the path. On his way, he spied the white sign that read *The Clark House Bed and Breakfast*.

Once inside the foyer, he gaped at the beauty of the place. Coffee-colored walls accented by mahogany wood trim extended to the high, vaulted ceilings. The floor was a dark hardwood, worn from age. He shivered, not because he was cold, but because he got the feeling he was being watched. Hanging on the wall to his right was a painting of a cemetery, and he wondered if it was the one across the street. In the background of the painting, a silhouette of a woman was portrayed. It was blurred but appeared as if it were meant to be a ghost.

"Here."

He turned to see the woman enter the room with a couple of towels. He noticed she'd removed her jacket and her shoes, and he drank in her natural beauty. Her brown hair fell to her waist like silk curtains. Around her neck hung a Sunstone wrapped in wire, dangling from a black leather cord. "Thank you."

As soon as he took the towels, she directed him to the stairs. "You can take room 15. From the top of the stairs, it's to your left at the end of the hall. There won't be any cell service due to the storm, and we don't have a landline. Breakfast is served between 7:00 and 9:00 AM." She frowned then added, "Never mind about breakfast. I let the staff have the weekend off so you're on your own. Sorry."

"The name is Nate Wilson, in case you need to keep a log of your guests," he stated as she turned to leave the room, not really meaning for her to respond. She seemed preoccupied.

When she faced him again, she frowned. The marble-size Sunstone hanging around her neck glowed briefly. Glowed? He shook his head. Maybe it had caught the light. Maybe he'd hit his head harder than he thought.

"I'm sorry. It's late. I didn't mean to be rude." She averted her gaze as if embarrassed by her actions. "Um, I'll make a note of it and we can clear everything up in the morning. You must be cold, plus you're dripping on the floor."

He glanced down and it was his turn to feel like a heel. "Right. Sorry, Ms..."

"Haylee. I'm the owner of the place. So if you need anything, I'm your girl. I'll let you get settled in. Have a good night, Mr. Wilson."

Haylee. He smiled, liking the sound of her name in his head, and watched how her hips swung slightly as she walked away. The idea of being stranded in a small town with her had brightened his mood. That was until he realized he'd left his suitcase in the truck of his car.

Great. He draped the towels over the stair railing before going back out to collect his things. As soon as he stepped out onto the walkway, lightning snapped overhead and thunder boomed. The rain fell in fat, heavy drops — faster than before.

By the time he returned to the house, he was soaked to the bone. His jeans stuck to his legs, and he sloshed with each step up the stairs. When he reached the landing and headed to his room, he noticed how quiet it was in the house. He couldn't be the only one there. Then he remembered Haylee mentioning that the staff was off. Did she mean she was closed?

Odd. Well, she was a little strange, as well. At least, her behavior was, going from being short with him one moment to apologizing the next. Maybe she was just shy. A smile tugged at his lips as he entered his room. He wanted to find out more about the beautiful, intriguing owner of The Clark House.

છૈ

A loud crash jolted Haylee upright in her bed. Her heart pounded as she tried to focus in the dim light filtering into her bedroom from the living room. She always kept the light on in there due to guests coming and going. But she only had one guest.

Reaching over to the nightstand, she felt around for her glasses, and then slid them on before getting out of bed. She grabbed her robe off the chair in front of her dresser on the way out the door.

Tying the sash, she noticed her guest, Nate, bent over. His lean, muscular, and shirtless back flexed as he stretched to pick up something from the floor. Warmth she'd never experienced before filled her. Then she realized she was ogling the man. No. She couldn't get involved with him or anyone.

Romance was off limits for her. She fell too easily, cared too much. So men were out. She would not suffer a broken heart as her mother and grandmother had. All because of a family curse that caused the men they loved to die.

When she got within a few feet of him, he threw up his hand. "Don't come any closer. There's glass everywhere."

She glanced to the accent table against the wall a few feet from the entryway of the great room. The vase that had once held a dozen red roses wasn't on the table, but rather on the floor. In a million pieces. Glass, water, and roses littered the foyer. "What happened?"

Nate straightened and faced her. She had to force herself to stay put. He was fit and looking yummy in nothing but his jeans. *He's not for you, Haylee.*

"I'm not really sure. I stepped off the stairs and the vase fell." He drew his brows together and stared at the mess on the floor. "This may sound crazy, but I swear it was thrown by someone or something."

She pursed her lips. It'd been quiet around there for the past year. The tourists she counted on to keep the B&B busy had lessened. They came to experience the ghostly activities from Lafayette Cemetery across the street, but with the lack of noises and moving objects, rumors started circulating that the stories were all made up.

"No, it doesn't sound crazy." She moved to the supply closet under the stairs and pulled out the Wet Vac. Nate took the vacuum from her and proceeded to clean up the floor. "I can do that."

"You don't have shoes on."

She glanced at his feet and frowned. "Neither do you?"

He looked at her over his shoulder, one brow raised in challenge and his lips curved in a playful smile. "I'm already over here."

"Have it your way." A smile tugged at the corners of her lips and she watched him clean up the glass and water.

When he finished, he handed the dozen roses to her. "You really didn't have to do that." She offered again.

"I felt like it was my fault somehow."

"Don't. The ghosts don't like roses."

He stilled and stared at her. "Ghosts?"

"Yeah." From his questioning tone, she could tell he believed in spirits or had had an experience with them before. "You're not scared, are you?"

He smiled at her teasing. "Nope. So, that was a ghost that made me crash my car?"

"Possibly." It was strange that the spirits would show themselves. What was so special about that night? Oh, yeah. It was the first night of the full moon. Meeting Nate's stare, she found herself captivated by his chocolate brown depths. For the first time in years, she felt at ease with another. "Would you like some tea?"

He nodded. "I'd love some."

Just as they turned to the kitchen, a knock sounded on the front door. Wondering who it could be at the late hour, she answered it. Nate was at her back, like he expected an attack or something. The sense of security warmed her. *Remember the curse. I won't be responsible for his death.*

When she opened the door, an older gentleman who looked to be in his late sixties, his hat and coat soaked from the rain, greeted her. "Hello, miss. Do you have any vacancies?"

"Yes, please come in." She moved to the side. "What are you doing out in this storm?"

"Oh, just passing through." He removed his wet, leather trench coat.

Haylee took it from him and opened the coat closet a few feet from the door. After grabbing a hanger, she hung the coat on the outside of the door to dry. Facing the stranger, she noted how his clothes weren't wet. *Odd.* Then again, it was a full moon, and she lived across from a haunted cemetery. So she let it go. "We were about to have some tea. Would you like to join us?"

"Tea sounds nice." The man moved toward the living room like he had a purpose.

She glanced at Nate, who shrugged. Nibbling on her bottom lip to keep a laugh from coming out, she followed the man. When he turned toward her room, she called out to him. "Um, sir, the kitchen is this way."

He faced her, then glanced back at her room, then to the kitchen on the opposite side of the great room. "Yes. The kitchen. For tea."

Beside her, Nate chuckled as the man strolled past. Haylee let out a sigh. It was going to be a long night.

Nate watched Haylee from across the small oak table in the breakfast nook as she set the silver serving tray with a white floral ceramic teapot and matching cups in the center. Her black-rimmed glasses slid down her nose, and his fingers itched to push them up. She was pretty, in a natural, almost plain kind of way. So different from the women he was usually drawn to. However, something about her captivated him.

Yet, he could tell she wasn't aware how pretty she was. *Interesting*. Well, he'd have to show her.

"How long has this house been in your family?" the older man asked before sipping his tea.

Haylee stiffened beside him then began to fidget with her silver spoon, flipping it over from front to back, over and over. "It's been in my family since the eighteenth century."

Nate could tell she was uncomfortable for some reason. Even before the other man had asked about the house. She'd reached for her neckline several times as if she searched for the necklace she'd worn earlier but didn't have on at the moment. In hopes of steering the conversation away from her, Nate met the man's gaze. "What is your name?"

"Con." He lowered his gaze and his brows dipped. Uncertainty brushed against Nate's awareness as the older man fingered the handle of his teacup.

"Is Con short for something?" Nate studied him. His silver hair covered his ears and brushed his brows.

Con glanced at Nate then to Haylee. "Constantine. But please, call me Con."

Haylee smiled and placed a hand on his arm. "Welcome to The Clark House. Oh, I'll be right back." She jumped up and left the room.

Nate frowned, wondering where she had gone. Focusing back on Con, he asked, "How long are you here for?"

"Three days." It came out as a mumble, but Nate caught it.

Okay, he was definitely a man of few words. "Do you have family in the area?"

"No." Con stood and moved to the door as Haylee appeared in the doorway.

She frowned and shot Nate a curious glance before returning her attention to Con. Handing him a room key, she spoke softly, "I put you in room 10. It's the first room to your right at the top of the stairs."

When Con reached for his wallet, she stopped him with a hand on his arm. "No charge. I was thinking of closing to the public this weekend. Kind of like giving myself, and the staff, the weekend off."

Con put his wallet away and took the key. "Thank you, miss." Then he left.

Haylee met Nate's stare. "He's a little strange."

Nate chuckled. "Yeah, just a little."

She laughed, the sound enveloping Nate like a lover's caress. He reached out to touch her cheek, but she backed away before he made contact. "Um, it's late and I should get to bed. I mean, go to sleep. With the staff off, I have to get up early. Good night."

A smile lifted the corners of his lips as he watched her flee from the kitchen and disappear into the living room. He was a believer that things happened for a reason. He was meant to be here, had to be. And the reason had just closed herself in her bedroom.

With purpose, he turned to the stairs just as a cold sensation went up his spine and skittered across his flesh. *What the...* He glanced to the top of the stairs and swore he saw a woman in white dart off to the right, toward Con's room.

When Nate reached the second floor, she was gone. He went to Con's door and listened. No sound came from the room. Shaking his head, Nate made his way to his own room. The stress from his job was finally taking its toll. He was losing his mind and, apparently, seeing ghosts.

Chapter Two

Haylee stepped out of the shower and sighed. The cool sprays of water hadn't helped her wake up. She hadn't slept well. Thoughts of the handsome, blond-haired, brown-eyed guest in the room above hers haunted her dreams. The whole time they had sat in the kitchen drinking tea, she couldn't stop the hum of desire racing inside of her. He made her nervous and turned her on at the same time. Something she couldn't afford to experience.

She'd never had a problem avoiding men before, but none had ever made her want things like Nate did. None had ever appealed to her like he did. And so fast.

Stop. You can't fall for him.

After quickly dressing, she slipped the Sunstone necklace over her neck. Once in place, she calmed, all feelings of hunting down Nate muted. Her whole body seemed to relax. A year ago, after her grandmother passed, Haylee had found the necklace among her Grams' things, wrapped in a black cloth. The stone always helped her relax and made her feel safe in an odd emotionless way. Plus, it made her feel close to her Grams.

She grabbed a hair scrunchy on the way out of her bedroom and twisted her hair up into a messy bun. Purpose — avoiding Nate — heavy in her thoughts. When she stepped out of her bedroom, the smell of coffee drifted in the air. *Mmm.* She inhaled the rich aroma and almost groaned.

Entering the kitchen, she frowned. Standing in front of the open refrigerator, Nate stared into it as if unsure what to pull out. She took her bottom lip between her teeth to keep from smiling. After a moment of ogling his backside, she asked, "What are you doing?"

He spun around to face her, his eyes narrowing slightly before his lips lifted at the corners. She waited for the desire she'd felt the night before to rise up. But it didn't. At least not as heavily as it had before she'd fled to her room. Like a coward. Last night, she'd all but undressed him with her eyes. However, at that moment, she didn't have the urge to be with him.

"I was going to fix you breakfast, then realized I don't know what you like."

"Why would you do that?" Her frown deepened. The gesture was sweet and a little romantic, yet her heart didn't flutter, and the butterflies in her belly were definitely sleeping in.

He moved closer to her. "Because I'd like to."

"Well, you don't have to. I'm capable of getting my own food." She brushed by him and took a muffin from the cake stand, then moved to the coffee maker. "I don't eat a whole lot in the mornings."

Coming up beside her, he took the cup she pulled from the cabinet and poured coffee in it. "What're your plans for today?"

She stared at him. Confusion clouded her mind, followed by annoyance. His tone hinted that if she didn't have plans, he did — for both of them. "Actually, I have a lot to do."

When she turned to leave, he gripped her elbow gently. Warmth seeped into her skin and she locked gazes with him, waiting for the spark from the night before. For a brief moment, she felt it, then he lowered his gaze to her necklace and frowned. The warmth and hint of desire vanished. "Does the stone always glow like that?"

"Huh?" She stepped back and glanced down. The Sunstone was glowing. Odd. "No." Wrapping her hand around the stone, she shook out of whatever fog she'd entered a moment ago. She couldn't allow the man into her life. The family curse would kill him. "I was able to get enough of a signal on my cell to send a message to the town mechanic. Hopefully, he'll have your car towed to his shop soon."

Nate drew his brows together but quickly smoothed them. "Thank you. Can I ask you another favor?"

"You can ask."

A soft chuckle escaped him. "Can I have a tour of the house?"

Oh. She relaxed some of the tension in her shoulders. "Where would you like to start?"

"You tell me." His lips lifted in a sensual smile she was sure would send any woman to her knees. Too bad hers didn't turn to jelly. Not that she wanted them to or anything.

"Well, I need to get a few items from the basement so we can start there." She crossed the kitchen to the door tucked in the far corner that opened the basement stairs. Glancing over her shoulder, she narrowed her gaze at Nate, who hadn't moved to follow her. "What's wrong? Scared of a little basement?"

The taunt drew another brilliant smile from him. "I was just admiring the view."

She rolled her eyes, even though she'd enjoyed the compliment, then opened the door and flipped the light on. It didn't matter that she'd lived her whole life in the house; the basement was creepy, even with the lights on. Stifling a shiver, she descended the stairs. A soft creak on the steps behind made her relax a little. Nate was there.

Stepping off the last step, she pointed to a shelf to the left where she stored the wine. "Can you grab a bottle of red?"

Nate did as she asked. She smiled. He really was a nice guy. Too bad he wasn't her type. She stilled then glanced at him from over her shoulder. Frowning, she couldn't remember what her type was. *Because you don't have a type. Family curse, remember?*

The stone around her neck warmed against her chest. Absently, she wrapped her fingers around it and turned back to finding something for dinner. With the staff off, it was up to her to cook. One of the few things she didn't care for, but she couldn't let her two guests starve.

"Does the house have hidden rooms?"

She thought about it for a moment then shook her head. "No, why?"

"I think you need to come look at this."

Okay. She crossed the room and frowned when he pulled the shelf away from the wall, taking a section of the bricks with it, like a door. "What the…"

Behind the wall, was an old wooden door coated in some kind of black grime. Reaching out, she touched the wood with her finger. That wasn't grime or dirt but something much darker. Black magic. She felt the heavy, inky energy reach out to her, twining around her wrist. The Sunstone once again warmed against her skin. Whatever was behind that door was connected to the stone and possibly her past.

She gripped the doorknob and turned, but before she opened the door, Nate touched her arm then jerked his hand away. "What are you doing?"

"I'm going to see what's in there."

He rubbed his hand on his jeans, glanced at the Sunstone, and then stared at the door. "I have a bad feeling."

So did she. But there were secrets locked up in that room or whatever it was. "It's an old house. Are you scared?"

He raised a brow as if waiting for her to open the door. So that's just what she did. As soon as she twisted the knob and pushed the heavy door open, black smoke rolled from behind it, thick with dark magic. A shiver went up her spine and the hairs on the back of her neck stood on end. Yet she couldn't turn back, couldn't ignore the hunch that she was meant to find the room.

Pushing the door wide, she stared into the dark room, waiting for something to jump out at her. Now who was the scaredy-cat? She took a deep breath then exhaled a moment before she crossed the threshold. Nothing happened. Relief flooded her.

The strike of a match drew her attention to Nate. He'd lit two tapered candles she kept on the shelf above the wine. Smart man. He offered her one of the candles and asked, "What is this place?"

She released a sigh as she moved farther inside the room. The moment the glow of the candlelight chased away the darkness, she recognized her grandmother's ritual box and a number of tools scattered across the table. Haylee hadn't revealed she was a witch to anyone. Especially strangers. The residents of Lafayette knew but never talked about it out of fear of the town curse. It wasn't like Haylee could perform any threatening magic. The only thing she could do was weave spells for healing, good health, and perform the occasional locator spell.

"This room was my grandmother's ritual room." Why didn't she recall the room before that moment?

"As in, she was a witch?" Nate's tone was calm, but she could sense his hesitation to enter the room.

"You don't have to come in if you don't want. I'll just be a few moments." She sat the candle in a nearby holder and spoke the single word enchantment to light the rest of the candles in the chandelier hanging in the middle of the room. "*Illumino.*"

The room became bathed with soft light. She scanned her surroundings and frowned. Papers littered the floor. The altar table was knocked over, and tools, salt, and herbs were spilled everywhere. Notes of sulfur and rosemary lingered in the air. A spell gone wrong? Or something much darker?

Haylee turned to leave then caught a glimpse of a photo on the workbench. The subject was the Sunstone she wore around her neck. *Huh?* As she moved closer to the table and the photo, the stone heated again and started to glow. Her blood ran cold in her veins and a raspy, deep whisper spoke in her mind. "*Make him leave.*"

She glanced to Nate at the door. He watched her cautiously. She stared back, and a flash of a vision formed in her mind's eye. It was brief, just one frame of an image she didn't really understand. Nate held a bloody knife in his hand as he stood over a body. Anger, fear, and horror filled her. A need for revenge amplified the emotions. *Kill him.*

Shaking off the image and the whispers in her mind, she backed away from the bench and rushed to the door, pushing Nate out of the way. With a flick of her hand, she called to the element of air, stirring up a breeze to blow out the candles. Then she slammed the door shut behind her. She didn't dare look at Nate. Fear chilled her to the bone. But she wasn't sure if it was for his life or hers.

Something very evil had happened in that room. Until she found out what, no one was to go in there. "Don't go in there alone, and don't tell anyone about it."

"No problem. I'm not a witch, but there is something…creepy about it."

Yeah, creepy was an understatement. She grabbed his hand and tugged him up the stairs and out of the basement, her food and supplies forgotten. She'd deal with what she had in the kitchen or go shopping later.

For now, the basement was off limits. At least until she figured out what the hell was going on.

Chapter Three

Nate closed the door to the basement behind him as Haylee rushed through the kitchen into the living room. She was hiding something from him. The heavy energy, or whatever it was in that hidden room had felt evil, dark.

From his brief time with Brie, a witch he'd dated in college, he learned a good deal about magic and ghosts. He'd left the spirit talking and magic to Brie because he respected the unknown too much. Plus, he'd always been a careful person. *Don't do anything that can kill you.* And messing with forces he wasn't familiar with could kill him.

He entered the living room just as Haylee darted into her bedroom and slammed the door. Frowning, he took a few steps toward the closed entrance. Curiosity whirled in his mind. He wanted to find out what had her so upset.

The sound of footsteps from behind stopped him. Glancing over his shoulder, he spied the older man, Con, standing in the archway between the foyer and living room, also staring at the door to Haylee's room. His brows were bunched together but not in confusion. With knowledge? Impossible. The old man had been in his room when Nate had come down. Besides, he hadn't been anywhere near the basement.

"Is she okay?" Con asked after a moment.

Nate glanced back at the door. "Yeah. She's fine."

"Right," Con breathed out then added, "The stone will keep you apart."

When Nate turned to look where Con had stood, he was gone. What the hell did he mean? *Crazy old man.* Focusing back on Haylee's door, Nate straightened his spine and marched toward the room. She was going to explain what the hell was going on.

He knocked on the wood and waited. A few heartbeats later, she snatched the door open. She narrowed her eyes at him. "What?"

Her tart response made him raise a brow. The annoyance in the single word was a huge change from the woman he'd spent time with last night and the moments before they'd gone into the basement. "Are you all right?"

"I'm fine." She went to close the door but he stuck his foot in the way. "What are you doing?"

"What happened in that room?"

Fear flickered in her eyes briefly, making them go round before she narrowed them again. "Nothing. Just stay out of the basement."

He studied her for a few moments. Her hands fisted at her sides, and she refused to make eye contact with him. Arguing with her and demanding she tell him what she was hiding would only push her further away. What if she were in trouble? She'd admitted she was a witch. From the hesitant admission, he guessed she didn't tell many people. She could be hiding her heritage or just plain hiding from someone or something.

Taking a breath and exhaling slowly, he relaxed his stance to appear less threatening. "You promised me a tour of the house."

Her sensual mouth dipped in a frown. After lifting her gaze to his, she relaxed and said, "Give me a minute, please."

He nodded and stepped out of the doorway. That time, the door was shut with a soft click. Smiling, he moved to the French doors that led out to the garden patio. He stepped outside and breathed in the damp, cool air. It was still dreary, and the clouds looked like another storm was closing in, ready to render its wrath on the earth.

He shivered as the wind picked up, blowing fallen leaves around the patio. Shoving his hands into his jeans pockets, he moved to the edge of the pavers and scanned the garden and beyond. He stopped when he noted that he could see the cemetery from where he stood. It looked creepier in the daylight than it had the night before.

Movement from behind one of the tombstones in the back caught his eye. When he moved forward to try and get a better look, nothing was there. After a moment or two, he saw it — a transparent figure in a white gown. His heart quickened as he picked up his pace, not sure what he was going to do once he was face-to-face with the ghost.

When he reached the gate, a man appeared in front of him. Nate jumped and blinked, his heart dropping to his stomach while pounding in his throat.

"Sorry, I didn't mean to startle you," the man said then glanced to the cemetery before returning his gaze to Nate. "Yeah, it's haunted. The witch who cursed this town refuses to leave."

Nate wasn't sure what the man was talking about. One last glance to the cemetery proved Nate was losing his mind. He ran a hand through his hair and studied the man. He was a few inches shorter than Nate and wore mechanic's overalls. Haylee had said she'd called someone. Extending a hand to the man, Nate introduced himself. "Nate Wilson. You here for my car?"

Nodding, the man shook his hand. "Yep. Jacob Bush. I took a look before loading it on the truck and it doesn't look too bad. Hole in the radiator, broken headlight, and minor body damage. I should have it good as new in a couple of days, depending on how fast I can get the parts in."

Thunder rumbled in the distance, drawing Nate's attention to the darkening sky. "Looks like another round rolling in."

"Yep. Could I get the keys?"

Nate patted his pockets for the keys then pulled them out and handed them to Jacob. "Take good care of her. She's not much, but she's all I have."

Jacob laughed. "I hear ya. You going to stay here?" When Nate gave a short nod, Jacob added, "Good, I'll call Haylee when it's ready for pick-up."

"Thank you."

Jacob turned and rushed to the front of the house where his truck was parked on the shoulder of the road. He waved as he climbed in and drove off.

Large, heavy raindrops fell around Nate, leaving dark blotches on the pavers. Nate rushed to the double doors right before the bottom dropped out. Haylee entered the living room about the same time, her damp hair hanging loosely around her shoulders. Her blue gaze lifted and locked with his for a long moment before she glanced out the French doors. "I'm sorry for snapping at you earlier."

"Don't worry about it. I can come off as a jerk sometimes."

That drew a smile from her. "You are a terrible liar."

He shrugged and gave her his best attempt at a seductive smile. "I try."

She averted her gaze and frowned. "Um, I guess we're stuck inside today."

An awkward silence settled between them. She rocked from foot to foot as if thoughts of fleeing the room were swirling in her mind.

"Why do you hide that you're a witch?"

"I don't." She released a heavy sigh and hugged her waist while tapping her bare foot on the tiled floor. "I just don't volunteer the info. I don't practice the Craft anymore. Not since Grams died a year ago."

Shit. He fumbled for the right words to say, finally settling for a simple, "I'm sorry."

She threw her arms out, waving off his ill attempt at an apology. "I never dealt in black magic. No one in my family did. At least, nothing like what happened in that room." She pointed to the kitchen where the basement entrance was.

"What happened down there?"

Shaking her head over and over, she paced the living room. "I don't know. It's dark, stronger than anything I've ever felt. Almost demonic."

He closed the distance between them and gently gripped her arms. Pulling her to him, he spoke softly. "I'm not accusing you of creating it. But I think we released it. Whatever *it* is."

She closed her eyes briefly before locking gazes with him. "As much as I don't want to go down there, I need to know what type of spell created the energy so I can cleanse the house."

Fear darkened her eyes. His heart ached, and the urge to protect her from the world bloomed inside his soul. He caressed her cheek with his knuckles. As soon as he made contact, the Sunstone around her neck glowed. Then she shoved him hard enough that he stumbled back a few steps.

"Don't touch me," she spoke in a low, growl-like tone before running out of the room.

The stone will keep you apart.

The old man's words drifted in Nate's mind. Yet, he didn't understand what it meant. Could the gemstone be influencing her mood? Impossible. Wasn't it?

Chapter Four

Haylee entered the library and shut the door behind her. Gods, she hoped Nate didn't follow her. The man confused her, irritated her. The way he smelled, his handsome face, and the sound of his voice both turned her on and made her want to kill him.

The latter scared the shit out of her. She was an earth witch. Positive, grounded, and loved all living things. The thought of harming another person made her ill.

She'd never wanted to hurt another. As least, not until she'd walked into that room.

Grams, what did you do?

With quick steps, she crossed the room to the middle of the bookcase, then turned the A and L volumes of the set of encyclopedias on their spines. A moment later, a section of the bookcase opened, revealing a small, square safe in the wall. After opening it and pulling out a thick folder, she sat in the chair at the mahogany desk a few feet to her left.

Anxiety made her hands shake as she touched the folder. She hadn't had a chance to read her grandmother's notes. She'd planned to add them to the family's Book of Shadows. At least the most recent one — it hadn't been updated in years. Since Grams was no longer with her, it was up to Haylee to keep the family history up-to-date so it could be passed along to future generations.

The inspiration to do so was lost on her. She was, after all, the only Clark witch alive. With the family curse hanging over her head, she wasn't about to find a husband and have children. She wouldn't marry without love, and she couldn't fall in love without sealing her husband's fate — to die.

Squeezing her eyes shut, she took a deep, cleansing breath. She really had to get a grip on her emotions. After opening her eyes, she cracked the folder without a clue of what she was looking for.

The curse. Grams could have been trying to break it.

With a direction, she scanned the first page of notes then turned to the next as the door to the library opened. Cutting a glare to Nate, she watched as he pulled a chair up to the desk and sat across from her.

She tried to ignore him and focus back on Grams' notes; however, the scent of sage from the soap she stocked in the upstairs bathrooms drifted from him, mingling with his own natural scent. The man was impossible to ignore. "Are you afraid of magic, witchcraft?"

"No. I'm not the type of person to fear the unknown. Although I did date a witch in college briefly." He leaned over the desk to peek at the contents of the folder.

Haylee lifted her gaze to his. Eyes the color of milk chocolate locked with hers. Compassion and a sense of a pure soul reached out to her. Nate got more interesting the more she got to know him. "A witch, really? What kind of witch was she?"

His brows bunched and he pressed his lips into a thin line before answering. "She was a hedge witch."

"Ah. No wonder you aren't surprised by ghosts."

A soft chuckle escaped him. "She was like a magnet for spirits. Anyway, it was a short relationship. Can we talk about something else?"

He did seem uncomfortable about the subject. She wondered if it had ended badly, or maybe the witch had just been using him. The latter happened too often, unfortunately. Witches were very selective in their life-long mates. So, she changed the subject as he requested. "Would you like to help me look for whatever my Grams did in that room?"

He nodded, his mouth lifting at the corners. "I don't have anything better to do."

She pressed her lips together to keep from smiling like an idiot. Nate made her giddy like a schoolgirl. His boyish charm and handsome features were all too easy to fall for. Shaking out of the dangerous train of thought, she focused back on the task at hand. After dividing the stack of papers in the folder, she handed him the top half. "I'm not a hundred percent sure what we're looking for. But a start would be information on a family curse."

"A family curse?"

As much as she didn't want to get into her family history, she needed his help to find answers as quickly as they could. The energy in the house grew darker by the moment, and it weighed on her. "The women in my family are cursed. All the men we fall in love with die."

And that was all he needed to know. For the moment anyway.

"So you've never been in love?"

She sat back in the chair and glared at him. "What about you?"

He shrugged and shifted the papers in front of him. "I was, once. Or at least I thought I was." His brows dipped and his lips thinned. "But that was a long time ago."

His tone as he spoke the last statement told her he was still a little bitter about the break-up. Curious, she couldn't help but ask, "What happened?"

A muscle in his left temple flexed. "I caught her screwing a co-worker in the bathroom."

"Oh, that's...I'm sorry."

"Don't be. It's over." He waved it off and changed the subject back to her. "You didn't answer my question. Have you ever been in love?"

Stifling a groan, she sat up and leaned closer to the desk, staring at the pile of papers but not really focusing on anything. "No." When he didn't comment right away, she asked, "What brings you to Lafayette?"

One shoulder lifted in a half-hearted shrug. "I was heading to the coast from California for a much-needed vacation."

"That sounds lovely. Are you meeting someone there?" Her chest tightened. She wasn't sure she wanted to know the answer to that question. Especially if he were meeting someone, like a girlfriend or wife.

Wait, why did she care? She couldn't get involved even if she wanted to. And the last thing Haylee needed was a relationship.

"No." He fell silent, drawing her attention to him.

A sense of loneliness drifted from him. "Are you running away?" She was half teasing, hoping to ease some of the tension between them.

He chuckled and met her gaze. "Actually, I am. Sort of. I'm bored with my job. And my life, I guess. I'm searching for a change, and hoped the ocean scenery would help me figure out what direction to go."

He was lonely and a little lost. She could totally relate. Although she had the B&B and loved managing the house and guests, she longed to share her life with someone. Fear of losing that person kept her at a distance from others, though. Never allowing herself to fall in love. It worked for her. Or so she'd thought before Nate crashed his car in front of her house.

"What do you do for work?"

He shrugged. "I'm Director of Finance for my father's business. It's a software development company."

There was something he wasn't saying, but she didn't pry. "Yeah, finance seems boring. I hire an accountant in town to keep my books for the inn. I love running the place, but hate the numbers."

"Finance and accounting have always been things I'm good at, but it's never been my passion."

She understood that. Magic ran in her veins, and she could perform spells as easily as breathing. Did she love the Craft? Not really. Maybe because of the curse hanging over her family for so long. "I get it. What *is* your passion?"

He glanced at her briefly. "It's nothing. I couldn't possibly ever do it."

Oh, now she was intrigued. "Tell me."

There was a long pause before he answered. "I've been working on a novel."

"Really? That's great. What is it about? Can I read it?"

He chuckled and shook his head. "It's a crime fiction book, and no, you can't read it."

She pretended to pout. However, she really did want to read it. "I love crime fiction."

He didn't answer her. Instead, he focused on going through the file contents. If he thought he was going to avoid it all together, he was wrong. When she opened her mouth to speak again, he said, "It doesn't matter anyway. I can't ever publish it."

"Why not?"

"My family is a little complicated. It's expected from birth that a Wilson child will work in the family business." He rolled his eyes before scanning over the papers again.

"That's crap. Your family will love you no matter what. I never really cared about the Craft, except for growing and using herbs. Anything magical just doesn't appeal to me. Grams told me that I'd found my talent in gardening and herbs. She never once forced me to cast spells or join in on rituals." Haylee couldn't imagine a family that would make each other miserable because they expected something. "Do your parents force you to work for the company?"

"Well, no. Yet no one in my family has never said they didn't want to."

"Until you?"

He nodded. "Yes. I feel like I'm letting them down."

Her heart ached a little for him. "I'm sure if you told them how you feel, they would understand. Plus, you don't have to quit your job to be a writer. Take a pen name."

When he didn't respond, she lifted her gaze to his. A shy smile lifted his lips. "You're right. I could write on weekends."

"And submit the book when you get it polished up?"

Nate watched Haylee as she turned her attention back to the stack of notes in front of her. Her statement churned in his mind. For too long, he'd put his own wants aside. And for what? He was afraid of letting his family down. However, Haylee didn't know how overbearing his family could be. "I'm not so sure about publishing. Right now, writing is just something to take my mind off real life."

"Maybe, but what would it hurt to casually mention it to your family." She didn't look at him as she spoke, and her tone was matter-of-fact.

Wanting to change the subject, he fell silent and searched through the notes, not really knowing for sure what he was looking for. A family curse, Haylee had said, but he didn't believe it. There was something else going on. And it didn't help that she hadn't told him everything.

"Tell me more about the curse." He straightened his stack of papers and pushed them across the desk.

She flicked a glance to him before combining the notes and shoving them into the folder. Her hands shook slightly. "All I know is that my grandpa and dad died because of the curse. Grams told me numerous times not to fall in love because we were cursed."

"And she didn't tell you why or how?"

She shrugged. "No. I asked all the time, and each time, she refused to tell me. As I got older, she grew more distant. She'd lock herself in the basement—now I know it was that ritual room—for hours, sometimes days."

"Then your answer could be in that room."

Glancing at the door of the library, she shook her head. "I know, but I was hoping to find something that hinted at what Grams was doing in there."

He cupped her hand with his, drawing her attention. "I'll go with you."

"Why?"

"I want to help you. Besides, I have nothing better to do until my car is fixed." He offered her a smile.

With her brows drawn together, she tugged her hand free and pushed away from the desk. The Sunstone around her neck glowed like it seemed to do whenever he was close to her. "Has the stone been in your family long?"

She touched the stone and stared down at him. "Yes, I believe so. My grandmother wore it for as long as I can remember…"

She trailed off, then her eyes grew round as if remembering something. He stood and placed his hands on the desk. "What is it?"

"Grams had worked in the ritual room for days. She'd forbidden me from entering the basement. When she finally came out, the stone was gone and she told me that everything would be fine now." Haylee hugged her waist as a single tear rolled down her cheek. "The next morning, I found her dead in her bed. She'd passed in her sleep."

Instantly, Nate rushed around the desk and wrapped his arms around her, drawing her into his chest. "I believe it's the stone that's cursed, not your family."

She lifted her head and locked gazes with him, her eyes narrowing. "The stone? Why the stone?"

"I'm not sure. But I think we need to find out." The first thing Nate would do was question the old man. After all, it was he who'd planted the idea in his head. "What do you know about it?"

"Grams found it when she and Papa were on vacation at the coast. The Sunstone can aid in healing, protection, and success. Plus, it's associated with the element fire, which was Grams' favorite element to work with." Haylee averted her gaze and moved toward the door, but not before he saw the tears fill her eyes.

"Is it possible that if the stone were cursed, it would react negatively?"

Stopping in the doorway, she turned to him. "Yes, that would, in many cases, be the point of a curse." She rushed out the room as if realizing something.

He followed her with quick steps, stopping when she entered her bedroom. "What is it?"

"It's just a thought, but I think Grams was trying the break the curse. When she was unable to, she tried to contain the negative energy." She zipped from her dresser to the nightstands on either side of her bed, opening drawers.

Confused, he watched her go to the closet and dig around on the floor. "I'm not following."

"If it is the stone that's cursed, then the fire within the stone is gone. The attraction and sexual energy were altered in some way. That is the only thing that makes senses." She pulled out a shoebox and opened it. A moment later, she withdrew a black cloth. After removing the Sunstone from around her neck, she wrapped it in the cloth and placed it inside the box. "Without the fire, the passion, a couple will fall out of love."

When she glanced up at him, tears rolled down her cheeks and she sagged into herself. The urge to comfort her was strong, yet he didn't know if she'd welcome it. The energy surrounding them seemed to darken.

From his time with Brie in college, he knew that witches mated for life. There was no divorce. The only way out of a loveless relationship was death.

"Grams and my mother killed their husbands," Haylee whispered, echoing his thoughts.

Chapter Five

Numbness filled every inch of her. Still, Haylee had to know for sure if the stone truly was responsible for her father's and grandfather's deaths. Replacing the lid of the shoebox, she returned it to the floor of her closet.

Without the Sunstone around her neck, she felt slightly lighter. At the same time, she could feel a dark pull to the stone. What did that mean?

And how the hell was she supposed to research the origins of a gemstone?

"Earlier, before you went to the library, Con said something that didn't make much sense to me at the time. But now I'm thinking he might be able to help us."

She glanced up at Nate's words, confused by how calm he was and that he actually wanted to help her. "What did he say?"

"'The stone will keep you apart.'" Nate frowned. "I'm still confused how he knows...never mind."

"He knows what?"

Nate shook his head. "It's not important right now. We need to figure out how to break the curse."

Crossing her arms, she glared at him. He raked a hand through his blond hair and sighed. When he met her stare, desire rushed through her veins like warm bath water before settling in her core. Like the night before, she wanted to touch him, taste him.

Oh, gods, it *was* the stone. But she couldn't think about getting involved with Nate. At least not until the curse was broken. "Forget it. Let's go find the old man."

She pushed past Nate and fought the urge grab him and drag him to the bed. What the hell was going on?

After crossing the living room, she climbed the stairs and went to Con's room. She knocked a few times with no answer. After a quick glance to Nate, she opened the door. The room was clean, and only one side of the bed was folded down. But there weren't any personal effects. No suitcase or clothes anywhere. He'd left? Without a word?

"Now what?" She turned to Nate and waited for him to tell her he had all the answers. He didn't. At least, not any she hadn't already thought of.

When she brushed past him to stand in the hallway, Nate gripped her elbow. "The ritual room is the only other option."

She knew that but had hoped the old man was still there to at least stall them long enough to postpone the trip to the evil room. "Okay, let's get it over with."

"We could just grab anything that looks like notes and go over them in the living room."

Nodding, she agreed. "Yes. That will probably be best. The less time I spend in that room, the better. At least, until I figure out how to cleanse it."

Fifteen minutes later, Haylee and Nate sat on the sofa with a couple of boxes of papers and books on the floor, one on either side of them. She wasn't sure what to grab, so she'd shoved every book, journal, and loose paper into boxes. The air in the ritual room had seemed darker than it had a few hours ago.

"Look for anything about the stone, the curse, confinement spells with notes, or anything that jumps out at you." She picked up a brown leather-bound journal from the box closest to her. *Please, Grams, give me a sign.*

"You said your grandmother died. What about your mother? Is she still alive?"

"No. She killed herself a few months after I was born. I grew up believing it was because she grieved for my dad. Now, I'm not sure." If the stone had pushed them apart and she'd killed her husband, then she wouldn't grieve. Would she? Maybe she felt guilty. Either way, she'd left Haylee.

Haylee's chest tightened and her eyes stung with tears. Pain she'd buried a long time ago rose again. She longed to know her mother, to feel her arms around her.

"I'm sorry. I didn't mean to upset you."

Out of reflex and the need to feel close to someone, she covered Nate's hand with hers. He lifted his gaze to hers, and she got lost in eyes that reminded her of melted chocolate. When he blinked, she shook her head then removed her hand. "You didn't upset me. My mother died, a long time ago."

He fell silent, which made her anxious. She needed noise or something to keep her mind from thinking about dark, evil curses. "What about you? Are your parents alive?"

"Yes, and they live in Florida. I haven't visited them in years, though."

"Do you have sisters and brothers?" she asked and picked up another book.

He shrugged. "Two brothers, both older than me."

"Ah, the baby of the family," she teased.

A chuckle rumbled from him and he leaned into her, bumping her with his shoulder. "You know it."

Laughing, she leaned back into him. A sense of comfort and kinship swirled around her. "What is it like to grow up with brothers?"

"It had its challenges and we fought a lot, but we are close. Being the youngest, I got blamed for a lot of stuff my brothers did. Mom always saw through it, though. When she couldn't, everyone got punished just so she knew she had the right one." He smiled as if the memories of his childhood were the best ones he had. And they probably were.

"That sounds great." Sadness and emptiness settled within. All she'd ever had was Grams. Now she was gone.

Nate covered her hand with his and squeezed. "What were you like as a kid? Wild?"

His teasing tone brought a smile to her lips. She playfully pushed him away from her. "No. Well, maybe a little. Like I said, I'm an earth witch, so being in nature is where I feel most comfortable. So I was always outside, playing in the woods or the cemetery."

She yawned and glanced at the grandfather clock next to the fireplace. "Wow, I didn't realize how late it was." They'd barely made a dent in their boxes.

Nate stood and held out his hand. "Come on, you need sleep. We can start again after breakfast."

Another yawn hit her and she nodded. "All right."

He walked her to her bedroom door, cupped her cheek, and kissed her. Shocked, she froze at first, not really believing what was happening. Once his tongue brushed against the seam of her lips, she opened. A moan escaped her, and she wrapped her arms around his neck, drinking in his scent and the feel of his body against hers. Tingles of desire fired off each nerve and she ached for more.

He broke the kiss and left her. She shouldn't get involved, but couldn't deny that she wanted him like no other. And it'd been too damn long since she'd had sex. Screw the damn curse.

She crossed the living room and climbed the stairs. She was going to enjoy every inch of Nate.

Nate had just tugged his shirt over his head and unbuttoned his jeans when a soft knock sounded on the door. A half smile lifted his mouth as he called out, "It's unlocked."

There were a few moments of hesitation before Haylee opened the door then closed it with a soft click behind her. When he faced her, she sucked in a breath, her gaze lowering to his impossibly hard cock, currently concealed behind denim.

When she didn't move, he held out his hand. "Come here."

She crossed the room and slid her hand in his, all the while locking gazes with him. There was so much uncertainty in her blue depths. With his free hand, he cupped her cheek, loving the way she sighed and leaned into the touch.

Closing the small space between them, he dipped his head to capture her lips. As soon as their lips touched, desire raced like wildfire through his veins. Need built inside him. His heart hammered as his skin grew sensitive.

Grabbing her ass, he lifted her off the ground and walked them to the bed. Instantly, she wrapped her legs around his waist, making each step painfully arousing. *Fuck*. He'd never felt so turned on, so alive from a kiss.

He lowered her to the bed and broke the kiss to trail his lips down her cheek to her neck. She groaned and tightened her legs around him. Slowly, he rocked into her, rubbing his erection against her core. Pleasure rippled through him and damn if he didn't almost come.

"Nate, I need you inside me."

She didn't have to tell him twice. He reached around and gripped her ankle gently. When she loosened her hold on him, he removed her jeans, taking her panties with them. Straightening, he removed his own jeans, then settled between her thighs. "Are you sure about this?"

One side of her mouth lifted as she hooked one leg around his, then flipped them over. She eased down, taking him fully. A hissed groan escaped him as she began to ride him. Slow at first, but when he gripped her hips, she picked up the tempo. Every muscle in his body tensed as pleasure built, fanning the flames of the wildfire she ignited inside him.

Above him, she tensed then shook slightly as she orgasmed, crying out in pleasure. Fisting a handful of her hair, he drew her down and claimed her lips. His balls tightened a moment before he fell over the edge of his own climax.

He held her warm, naked body close to his as the last shudders of their orgasms left them. Their heartbeats fell in sync for several moments, returning to their normal rhythms as the rush of passion melted away.

Haylee crawled off him and moved to the edge of the bed. He gripped her wrist. "Where are you going?"

She hesitated for several long moments before speaking. His gut burned with fear that she'd say it was all a mistake. A soft sigh escaped her. "I need a shower."

Sitting up, he leaned into her and kissed her cheek, letting his lips linger. "I'll come with you."

She shook her head a few times before she nodded. "Okay."

Before she had the chance to flee the room, he whispered, "I don't want this to be a one-nighter. We'll figure out the curse. We have to because I want to be with you for however long we're meant to be."

Her blue eyes met his. A smile lifted her lips. "I'd like that, but right now, I can't see a future until the curse is broken."

"Fair enough. First thing in the morning, we'll get to work on finding some answers." He stood and offered his hand. "How about that shower?"

A shy smile formed and she placed her hand in his. A renewed sense of purpose filled him. He had to help her solve the mystery of the cursed stone and win her heart at the same time. There wasn't a challenge he'd ever backed away from. He wouldn't start now.

Chapter Six

Haylee cradled her warm cup of coffee in her hands as she stepped out onto the patio. The sun was barely peeking over the horizon and it cast an orange glow behind the clouds. There was a slight chill in the air. Breathing in deeply, she welcomed the crisp, clean scents of the earth and took in the rising sun's energy.

Images of her and Nate from the night before whirled in her mind. Their tangled arms, legs, and bodies in his bed, the shower, against the bedroom door. A groan escaped her while the cold burn of fear crawled up her spine.

She hadn't known what to expect upon waking a few minutes ago. She'd watched him peacefully sleep for a few moments before coming downstairs. She expected to still be humming blissfully after the passion they'd shared. However, her desires for him had dulled, and that saddened her.

The curse. She ground her molars. That had to be it. The reason she'd wanted him one minute and wanted to flee him the next. The dark energy they'd released from the ritual room lingered in the house. And it felt darker, alive, like it was changing into an entity of some kind. It was draining, and it made her irritable.

It had to be stopped. She would break the curse if it were the last thing she did.

Turning around, she entered the living room, leaving the French doors open, and sat down in front of the box of Grams' journals and notes. There had to be something in there. After setting her cup on the coffee table, she pulled out a stack of loose notes. Most of the pages were recipes for teas and soups for healing and good health. Not one mentioned a curse or the Sunstone.

She let out a frustrated growl just as Nate entered the room. Meeting his narrowed-eyed gaze, she pursed her lips. Her first reaction was to be annoyed with him, but why? Taking a deep breath, she drank him in while pushing the negative emotions away. His hair was ruffled from sleep and he wore nothing but a pair of blue jeans.

Meeting her gaze, he motioned to the stack of papers. "Did you find anything yet?"

There was a slight edge to his voice, as if he were annoyed by her presence, as well. Crap. The curse was starting to affect his mood, too. This wasn't going to end well if she didn't figure out how to break the spell.

"No. You could help instead of standing there." She closed her eyes and tried to shove away to urge to throw something at him.

He was in front of her within moments, pulling her to a stand. His sensual lips lifted in a humorless smile. "We need to hurry. I woke this morning angry you weren't in the bed. I don't get upset over things like that. Now that I have, I'm not sure if I want to kill you or fuck you."

Oh, good gods. Liquid heat rose within her. Every part of her begged for the promise of being taken by him while her mind screamed to push him away. "Well, killing me won't break the curse."

"I guess that leaves the other option."

When he dipped his head, she pressed her finger to his lips. "Later. Right now we have notes to sift through." She stepped out of his embrace. "I'll make some tea that could help relax us enough to focus."

Her hands shook as she put the kettle of water on the stove. For the three minutes it took the water to heat, she focused on calming her emotions and being thankful she didn't have a psychic connection to the elements. Uncontrollable emotions would influence the weather. The last thing she needed was an out of control storm to deal with on top of this crazy curse.

The screaming of the kettle brought her out of her thoughts. Grabbing the chamomile and mint tea she'd mixed up the day before, she placed everything on a tray then headed to the living room.

Nate sat in the middle of the sofa, flipping through a journal. She sat the tray on the coffee table. "Have you seen Con?" Nate asked.

She poured his tea and handed the cup to him. "No. Here, drink this."

One brow raised suspiciously as he took the cup from her. He brought it to his nose and sniffed. Oh for the love of the gods. She snatched the cup, the warm liquid sloshing over one side, and took a sip. "See, not poisoned."

When she offered it back to him, he closed his eyes briefly and raked a hand through his hair — a gesture she'd come to realize meant he was riding high on emotions. "I don't know what's wrong with me."

She waved him off and sat by her box. "It's the energy in the house. It's changing somehow. Becoming darker."

They worked in silence for the next thirty or so minutes until she spotted the word "stone" in Grams' notes. Reading on, her heart dropped at seeing the words confirming what she and Nate suspected.

The stone is cursed. It's the only thing that makes sense. Ever since I found it on the beach, I felt the evil hidden inside it. Although, at the time, I didn't know it was the stone slowly poisoning my mind, and then Donna's once I gave it to her as a gift. It was Donna who figured it out. But I was too late to save her.

I tried to take the stone back to the beach, even tossed it in the ocean. But when I got home, it was sitting on my dresser again. I've come to the conclusion that once the stone is in a family's possession, it can't be given away or left somewhere until the whole line of females are destroyed. So, the only thing left is to figure out how to break the spell.

Haylee stopped reading and blinked away the tears. A moment later, Nate moved closer to her and gently slid the paper from her hand. When she lifted her gaze to him, his brows were bunched together. "Donna is my mother."

With a single nod, he reached over and linked his fingers with hers. She welcomed the comfort he offered. "She tried to break the stone." He released her hand and cupped her chin, lifted it so she'd meet his gaze. "According to your grandmother's notes, your mother didn't kill herself over grief or guilt. She tried to destroy the stone and died as a result."

Then why would Grams tell Haylee it had been suicide and that the family was cursed? She'd warned Haylee repeatedly not to seek a mate or fall in love, that the curse would leave her alone, bitter, and heartbroken for the rest of her life.

She wouldn't have lied to her.

Would she?

No.

Standing, Haylee shook her head and wrapped her arms around her waist. "This is too much. I need some air." She rushed out the French doors, through the back gate, and across the street to the cemetery.

Tears streamed down her face, turning into sobs as she fell to her knees in front of her mother's and grandmother's graves.

A folded piece of paper floated down, landing on Grams' headstone. After wiping the tears from her cheeks, she picked up the paper and glanced up. A woman dressed in a white gown and a green, hooded cloak stared at her from a few feet away. When Haylee stood, the woman faded away. A ghost. Odd.

She glanced down at the paper and unfolded it. In an elegant handwriting was what appeared to be some kind of short poem. At closer inspection, Haylee realized it wasn't a poem but a curse.

Stripped of fire and passion.

The Sunstone and those who possess it, lose all attraction.

See with the heart

To renew the spark.

Frowning, she churned the words around in her mind. She guessed the last part was how to break the curse, but she hadn't a clue what they meant. Maybe she and Nate could figure it out.

With renewed hope, she slipped the paper into her pocket and headed back to the house.

Haylee entered the backyard and stopped when she saw Nate standing on the patio, staring off into the empty pastures surrounding the house. "Is everything okay?"

He answered without looking at her. "The effects of the curse aren't as bad out here."

Coming to stand next to him, she felt it. The curse seemed to be contained within the house, closer to the stone. Linking hands with him, she tugged him farther away from the patio. Once they were outside the garden, she pulled out the slip of paper and handed it to him. "A ghost dropped this on Grams' headstone."

A frown formed on his face as he opened the note and read. "What does it mean?"

"I'm not sure, but I think the last part is how to break the curse." She paced, shaking her head. "But see *what* with the heart?"

"Love. Allow yourself to love wholeheartedly."

She faced him. "No. Everyone I've loved has died. And my mother killed her husband, whom according to Grams, she loved with every fiber of her soul."

Nate threaded his fingers through his hair. "So, what do we know? Your grandmother found the stone and her husband died. What about your parents? How did they meet and fall in love if they were around the stone?'

Haylee thought about it and remembered the story from reading her mother's journals that Grams had given her. "Mom and Dad met in college and were married during their junior year. Mom was six months pregnant with me when they graduated. Then they moved in with Grams."

Nate let out a soft curse and tugged her into a hug. "The curse destroyed everything they had."

"Mom killed Dad a month before I was born."

A sob escaped her and she wrapped her arms around Nate's waist. She pressed her cheek to his chest and allowed the steady rhythm of his heartbeat to soothe her. It was so easy to open up to him. It was as if they were meant to be together. Lifting her head, she met his gaze and knew what they needed to do. "It's us. We have to fight the pull of the curse and open our hearts."

"Love conquers all."

Love? She wasn't sure she knew what that was. Yet Nate fascinated her in a way no other had. She was definitely attracted to him as long as she stayed away from the Sunstone and fought the dark energy, keeping it from seeping into her. "So, where do we begin?"

Chapter Seven

For the first time in his life, he had a plan for the future. Not a whole plot, but a path had formed and he was going to walk down it.

Haylee blinked at him, innocence in her blue depths. She'd run from her passion and hidden her heart her entire life. It was time to get her to break open that shell. Nate was happy to assist.

Snaking an arm around her waist, he tugged her close until their bodies pressed together. "From the first time I saw you, I wanted to learn everything about you. To crack the wall around your heart. Every time one of us pushes away, the other will pull them back in. It's the only way I can think of to overcome the effects of the curse."

She sucked in a breath, her eyes closing as a soft moan escaped her. Then she opened them and stared into his. "What if opening our hearts isn't the answer?"

He pressed a finger to her lips. "Shh. We'll figure out something else."

"How can you be so sure?"

"Because for the first time in a long time, I know exactly what I want." He kissed her cheek then dragged his lips to her ear. "I want you."

"Oh, gods. Yes." It came out as a whisper as she melted into him.

He drew back a little, helped her steady herself, and then took her hand in his. "First, we need to do a little speed dating. Get to know each other."

With a shy smile, she said, "We could go on a picnic since the weather is nice at the moment."

"That sounds…nice." He wouldn't have chosen a picnic, but he'd go with it.

She narrowed her gaze at him. "Was that sarcasm?"

"Not at all. I like to eat. It doesn't matter how I do it."

She rolled her eyes and turned toward the house. "You know you can't lie to a witch, right? Not even a little bit."

A smile tugged at his lips and he followed her, watching how her hips swung as she moved. "Yeah, I know. I'm not a nature person. It's a flaw from living in a large city all my life."

She whirled around, stopping in his path. "That will change. Nature is my life and my connection to my magic, what little I have."

"You are stronger than you think." He kissed her quickly on the lips.

"I hope you're right." She frowned before heading back to the house.

He caught up with her within a few steps and linked their fingers. His warmth wrapped around her, protective and caring. The walls around her heart started to crumble.

In the kitchen, she pointed to the pantry. "Can you grab the basket from the top shelf? I'll start the sandwiches."

He nodded and did as she asked. "I could get used to this."

She froze briefly then proceeded to pull slices of bread out. "Used to what?"

"Being here, with you." He chuckled as if he'd thought of something funny. "Is it strange that I feel so comfortable with you?"

He sat the basket on the counter next to her. She glanced at him then met his chocolate stare. "No. I mean it's unusual for me." People met all the time and fell in love, didn't they?

Although what they had wasn't love. She frowned. But they needed it to be to break the curse. "I don't see how this is going to work."

She left the kitchen and headed to her room. Sadness swallowed her and cast her into a pit of loneliness and desperation. When she'd reached her bedroom, Nate caught up with her. He grabbed her arm and twisted her hard enough for her back to hit the closed door. She gasped, but his mouth taking hers in a searing hot kiss muffled the sound.

Desire and a need to be possessed by him overtook her. She threaded her fingers in his hair and fisted a handful. A moan vibrated from his chest and throat. He tightened his hold on her and pressed his hard, jean-covered cock into her abdomen.

All thoughts of fleeing him and the curse faded, replaced by the desire to find a way to break down the walls that kept her from opening up to him. She broke the kiss and hugged him. "It's going to be a fight."

"Yes. But the curse seems to be more directed at you."

She shrugged and stepped out of his embrace to sit on the floor in front of the fireplace. With a thought, she invoked the fire spell Grams had taught her. It was similar to lighting the candles, but instead of a word of Latin, she used her will to envision the logs in the hearth ignited. A moment later, orange and red flames flared to life.

Nate sat beside her, stretched out his legs in front of him, and crossed his ankles. "I thought you said you didn't have magic."

She laughed at the playfulness in his tone. "I said I had little magic. Most witches can perform minor telekinetic skills that deal with the elements. Some can even move objects. Before you ask, I cannot move objects."

"And yet, I still like you." He grabbed her by the waist and pulled her to the floor. She let out a squeak then laughed as he hovered over her. His sensual lips lifted at the corners. Suddenly, he frowned and rolled to his back.

Emptiness crept in, surrounding her heart like a vise. *Stop. It's the curse and the building evil in the house.* She took his hand and relaxed when he gave a gentle squeeze. "What is it like living in the city?"

"There are a lot of large buildings and very little trees."

"That sounds horrible."

He laughed, the sound masculine and husky. "I didn't know of any other life."

Turning to her side, she studied his profile. His nose was slightly bent. "That makes sense so I forgive you."

The corner of his mouth lifted before he turned to his side to face her. "I like this playful side you."

So did she. It felt good to just open up and let someone into her life. Especially after spending the last year alone and grieving. Nate was perfect in an imperfect way. He could make her forget the whole world existed. "I like that you bring it out in me."

He kissed her and let his lips linger on hers. A sense of peace and acceptance settled inside her. When he drew back and smiled, she knew he was hers. He was worth fighting for. "Nate, I…"

The dark energy moved in around them. No, around *her*, trying to divide them. She tried to speak, to say the words on her tongue, but nothing came. A moment later, her breathing came in gasps. What felt like hands around her neck tightened, making it impossible to speak or breathe.

She rolled to her back and clawed at her throat, fighting to draw in air. Nate scooped her up in his arms. Her surroundings rushed by, then fresh, crisp air hit her.

"Breathe for me."

Nate's shaky words cut through the fog. Another moment passed and she began to breathe. She coughed a few times before she was able to speak. "What?"

"Shh. Don't talk. Just breathe." Nate hugged her to him. She could feel his heart beating rapidly in his chest.

She didn't know how long they sat in the middle of the garden in each other's arms before she finally broke the silence. "I don't understand. I thought if I opened my heart and admitted that I'm falling in love with you, the curse would break."

"The words might not be enough, or we unleashed something far more evil than we thought." He paused then his eyes lit up with realization. "You're falling in love with me?"

She nodded, able to think clearer outside. "For a moment, I saw what could be between us and I wanted it. And I'll fight to get it."

Chapter Eight

Nate had just dried the last dinner plate and placed it in the cupboard when the hairs on his arms and the back of his neck stood on end. The air around him chilled, and a gust of a breeze rushed by him. Glancing at the window, he confirmed it was shut and there were no others in the kitchen. He ground his molars. Since the incident that afternoon with Haylee, the dark force in the house had gone quiet.

It seemed it was getting ready to play some more.

A dark presence, stronger than the one he'd felt in the basement when he and Haylee had opened that hidden door, moved in behind him. Turning, he scanned the room and found nothing. Then the basement door *creaked* open. Narrowing his eyes, he crossed the kitchen and slammed the door shut.

"What is it?"

His heart hammered against his ribs as he jumped and whirled around, falling into a defensive stance. Haylee stood in the archway of the foyer, her brows raised in question. Relaxing, he shook his head. "The basement door was open an…"

She flicked her gaze to the door. "I felt the energy, too. It's different than before, stronger."

They needed to find a way to stop it. "Do you think your grandmother wrote down the spell she used?"

Haylee frowned but nodded. "Yeah, she wrote everything down. It'd be in one of the boxes."

With a last look at the basement door, he left the room, not wanting to be around it any longer. He settled on the sofa and picked up a handful of papers. A moment later, Haylee came in and sat in the chair across from him. She'd moved her box with her.

Setting the papers back in the box, he rose and went over to her and held out his hand. Reluctantly, she took it and he tugged her to a stand. Since the evil had tried to choke her, she'd been a little distant. He couldn't blame her. He cupped her cheek, drawing her gaze to his. "You're beautiful."

A laugh bubbled from her and she averted her gaze. "Thank you." She hugged him, shaking as she did. "I don't like the dark thoughts I have. I don't like the fear of what will happen if I'm close to you."

"The fear is what will keep us apart." He tightened his hold on her, loving the feel of her in his arms. He was falling in love with her. "We'll figure this out."

She nodded and stepped out of his embrace. "We need to find that containment spell. Then pray to the gods I can recreate it."

"You will." He picked up the stack of papers again and began to sift through them. "What if we don't find it?"

"Hush. We need to focus on the positive."

That was easier said than done. But she was right. Negative fed negative.

Nate picked up the last sheet from the box and frowned. They'd been searching all night and...nothing. Damn it. There had to be an answer somewhere.

"I think I found it."

He jumped up and rushed to her side. When he reached her, he was thrown across the room. He landed on his ass and slid into the wall. Haylee ran to his side. "Are you all right?"

"Yeah. At least we know it isn't picky on who it attacks." He eased to his feet, a dull pain shooting up his back. "Please tell me you found the containment spell."

"Yep, and there is a vanquishing spell attached to it."

"Vanquishing? Like for a demon?"

She moved back to her seat and picked up the journal. "Yeah, but it looks unfinished."

The air around them thickened, almost shocking. He closed in on Haylee as she read her grandmother's notes. For some reason, the entity or whatever it was didn't leave the house. "Let's go out on the patio."

Haylee nodded and walked to the French doors. "It would be better. I'll need some things from the garden anyway."

Once outside, the heaviness lifted and he could breathe easier. The creak of the gate caught his attention. After a sharp glance, expecting something to come at him, he relaxed at the sight of Con entering the backyard.

The old man met his stare with his own haunted gaze. Dark circles under the man's eyes hinted that Con was tired. Nate couldn't shake the feeling that the other man had seen much more than one lifetime could offer. "We thought you left."

Con stopped at the edge of the patio, staring at the house. "I had a few things to do."

Haylee pushed past Nate to get to Con. Wrapping her arm around his, she tugged him to the small wicker sofa. "You look tired."

Con smiled but it didn't reach his eyes. "Not as tired as you."

"That might be true, but I have youth cn my side."

As soon as Con settled in his place on the sofa, Nate said, "You knew the stone was cursed."

Haylee whirled around to face him, narrowing her eyes. "Nate."

Con placed a hand on Haylee's forearm. "I didn't know at first. Not until I saw the stone before I slipped out."

"When was this?" Suspicion crawled up Nate's spine as he glared at the old man. The feeling that Con was hiding something or knew more than he let on settled in the pit of Nate's gut.

"Yesterday morning. You two were in the living room and too focused on each other." Con shivered and glanced over his shoulder to the French doors. "Something has changed."

Haylee hugged her waist. "I believe we may have freed an evil ghost. Or something darker." After she had taken a deep breath, she stared at Con. "What do you know about the curse?"

"I'm not certain, but I believe it is connected to my own curse."

"You're cursed?" Nate and Haylee asked at the same time. Nate stepped closer to Haylee, the need to protect her strong.

Con gave a single nod before a shimmer of magic rippled around him. Then his appearance changed from an old man to a young, thirty-something man. His light brown hair fell to his shoulders, framing his face. He wore a chainmail cowl over a tunic. A knight? From the cross on the front of the tunic, Nate guessed Con had been in the Crusades, which meant the man was *really* old. "When were you cursed?"

Glancing down at himself, Con frowned. "1169 AD. What year is it?"

"2016," Haylee said softly. "Why were you cursed?"

Con lifted his gaze to Haylee then to Nate. "I fell in love." A shadow passed over Con's features and his eyes shone with unshed tears. His voice cracked as he spoke. "Amara, my one true love, had been promised to another. Her father made a deal with a demon in exchange for power and riches. When the demon found out Amara and I had fallen in love, he lashed out in a jealous rage, cursing us both. I'm cursed to only walk as a man during the three days and nights of the full moon's light. Each full moon, I'm transported to a different pace, but I didn't know why until I came here. I'm meant to find the Sunstone."

"What happened to Amara?"

"I don't know." Con stood and walked toward the garden to their left. "The energy in this house feels like the demon's."

Nate thought back to when they'd opened the door in the basement, the *whoosh* of demonic evil when the seal had broken and the charge within the room that had made his skin crawl. "Do you think your curse and the curse on the stone are related?"

Glancing over his shoulder, Con stared at him, sorrow still heavy in his gaze. "It's a theory. I feel in my heart that I'm meant to be here to help the two of you break the curse. Or at least it makes sense according to my own curse. However, Haylee's grandmother opened something up when she tried to break the curse with a spell."

Beside Nate, Haylee shuddered and turned her head to peer toward the kitchen. "If the Sunstone is connected to the demon or the curse, it could be that Grams summoned him. When she couldn't banish him, she sealed the room with him in there."

Dread hit Nate like a truckload of bricks. "When we opened the door, we released him."

Con faced them and straightened his shoulders. "You must reseal the room with him in it before the curse can be broken."

Nate looked at Haylee. "You can do that, right?"

Her eyes grew round then she drew her brows together. "I'm...I'm not sure."

Taking her hands in his, Nate locked gazes with her. "I believe you can. I'll be there with you."

She shook her head. "It's too risky for you to be there."

He cupped her chin. There was no way she was going to do it alone. "I want to be there, to help you in any way I can. I'm not going to take no for an answer."

His last statement drew a small smile from her. "Do as I say. I don't need to worry about you. Especially after the aggression the demon showed to you earlier."

Leaning in, he quickly kissed her then said, "Yes, ma'am."

Chapter Nine

Haylee knelt in her closet and stared into her ritual box. Taking slow, deep breaths, she willed the fear of failure away. She hadn't created or crafted a spell since she was nine, when she'd killed her best friend at the time. The horror of what she did to Mary had crippled Haylee's ability to effectively perform spells.

Old pain rose up, gripping her heart and squeezing it. Tears welled up in her eyes, but she blinked them away.

After picking up a jar of salt and a vial of blessed water, she clutched them to her chest. *Come on, get up.* She was the only one who could cast the containment spell.

The slight creek of the bedroom door caught her attention. She glanced to Nate, standing in the doorway. He gave her a reassuring smile, yet a hint of concern showed in his eyes. "Are you okay?"

"No." she glanced down at the items in her hands. "I killed my best friend."

The hardwood floors groaned under Nate's tennis shoes as he moved closer. "What happened?"

There was no accusation in his tone, just a question from a concerned friend. Her heart melted at the thought. He really did care for her. "We were playing in the woods surrounding the cemetery. I climbed a tree, and Mary was afraid she'd fall. So I did a levitation spell and lifted her up in the tree." Tears stung her eyes. When Nate tugged her to him and hugged her tight, she wrapped her arms around him, welcoming his comfort. "She sat on the branch with me, laughing as we talked about the boys from school. Then she fell. She broke her neck and died instantly."

Nate threaded his fingers into her hair and held her a little tighter. His lips pressed against her temple. "It was an accident."

"I used magic to get her in the tree. If I hadn't, she never would have gone up. It was my fault."

He framed her face and forced her to look into his eyes. "You were kids. Besides, you didn't use magic to make her fall." He paused, but before she had a chance to speak, he added, "I had a younger sister. Casey. She was really only a baby at five years old. I was supposed to watch her, but a friend came over and I went out of the house to talk with him. Casey was in her room. When I came back inside and checked on her, she was face down in the tub. I guessed that she wanted to take a bath so she'd turned on the water. It was still running when I reached her."

His voice cracked. Haylee lifted her gaze. "It was an accident."

"I was supposed to watch her. Besides, I left the bathroom door open; something my mom yelled at us boys about every day once Casey learned how to turn the water on. I watched my mother crumble when she found out." He sniffed, and Haylee wiped a tear from the corner of his right eye.

"I'm sorry." She didn't know what else to say. His pain reached out to hers, mingling. In that moment, their auras shifted to a dark blue, blending into each other like waves in the ocean.

He placed a finger under her chin and lifted. Their gazes locked, and for the first time since he'd walked into her life three days ago, she truly saw him with her heart. "Casey was an accident. It took me a long time to believe that. Even though I got in trouble for not watching her like I should have, I wasn't blamed for her death. I never understood why. It was my mother who helped me see it. She told me that things happen for a reason. No one, not even she, could possibly watch Casey every hour of the day."

A frown pulled at Haylee's lips. Mary's fall wasn't Haylee's fault. She knew that but couldn't help feeling responsible. Even if it was she who pointed the finger at herself.

Her magic didn't fail her, her fear had. Straightening her spine and stepping back, she lifted her hands with the salt and water and said, "We have a demon to contain."

They walked to the basement in silence. Con had opted to wait in the living room, muttering something about not being too involved. Involved in what, exactly, she didn't know. The ritual? Maybe. But Haylee didn't care either way. She didn't need the extra body in her way.

After opening the door to the basement, she took a deep breath. "We need to get the demon inside the room. One he's there, we need to get out so we aren't trapped in there with him." She met Nate's stare. "When I say leave the room, you leave."

"No problem." He frowned as he caressed her cheek.

She sighed and leaned into him. Warmth enveloped her and her chest tightened. *Please, gods, give me the strength needed to face what is to come.* "Let's do this."

The hairs on the back of her neck stood to attention. Dark magic closed in on them. It was time to move. She'd already begun to open her heart to Nate, which had angered the demon. She felt it. The energy had strengthened, becoming thicker, like tar.

She descended the stairs and hurried to the ritual room behind the metal shelves. Nate was on her heels, and from the way he stayed close to her, she guessed he too could feel the demon following them.

This was too easy.

She banished the thought and focused on the positive. They would succeed. They had to.

When Nate stopped and faced her, she kissed him. Instantly, he gripped her hips and drew her closer, meshing their bodies together. His erection pressed into her abdomen and she ached to have him inside her.

She broke the kiss on a gasp as dark magic nipped at her skin as if punishing her for falling in love with Nate. The demon's essence swirled around them, growing darker by the minute. Emotion fueled his demonic power. For a brief moment, she could feel him. It was as if his physical form were trapped somewhere and his spirit searched for a way to free itself.

"Run," she whispered to Nate and then ran to the door. Nate was on her heels but when she reached the doorway, Nate wasn't there. She turned in time to see him fly across the room and slam into the far wall. She screamed and wished she had natural power to fight the demon.

As soon as she moved to rush to Nate's side, she was thrown out of the room, landing on her ass and sliding into a cabinet she kept dry foods in. Then the door to the ritual room slammed shut.

"No! Nate!" She pushed to a stand and grit through the sharp pain shooting from her hip down her leg. Footsteps stomping down the stairs made her whirl around, ready to fight whatever she had to in order to get Nate back.

Con held his hands up. "What happened?"

"The demon has Nate in there."

"He's trying to keep you two apart."

Yeah, she'd guessed that much. "We need to get Nate out of there. He's hurt."

Her heart ached as she stared at the closed door that trapped her...her what? Her soul mate?

"You're in love with him." Con's tone was soft and held a hint of hope. He grabbed her hand and tugged her up the basement stairs. "I know what we need to do."

Haylee paced the living room with the Sunstone in hand. Con's plan churned in her mind. After several moments of convincing, she'd retrieved the stone from her ritual box, not completely sure she wanted to be near it. But Con had made a point.

"Your grandmother somehow summoned the demon with the stone. So you will do the same thing, but into a circle, contain him, and then banish him from this house." Con paced to the French doors and glanced outside. "And this needs to be done before the moon rises."

Haylee nodded. This was the last day Con would be with them. When the moon rose he would become a gargoyle until the next full moon. "Okay." She took a deep breath and exhaled slowly.

Closing her eyes, she reached out her senses to the elements for guidance and strength. She opened her eyes and picked up the salt from the mantel and drew a large circle in the center of the living room, which was free of all furniture. Once the circle was complete, she exchanged the salt for the blessed water. From her grandmother's notes, she'd discovered that all she had to do was trap the demon and order him to leave the house while spraying the water on him. *Sounds easy enough.* She rolled her eyes at her own sarcasm.

It would work. She was going to free Nate or die trying.

She backed up a few feet from the circle and held out her hand, palm up, with the Sunstone in it. "I summon the demon within these walls."

The stone warmed in her hand, then heated to the point it burned her hand. She could barely hear Con behind her saying not to drop the stone. She pushed through the pain and focused on the demonic energy. "I summon you within my circle. Face your fate. Face me."

A moment later, a dark shadow of a man formed inside the circle. A deep growl cut through the air and echoed throughout the house. The demon had long, black hair and wore dark clothes. She couldn't make out his facial features very well, most likely because he was not there in physical form.

How was she to throw water on him if he was a spirit? If he was connected to the stone, as they believed, she could use it. Hell, she'd try both the stone and the shadow of the demon. Picking up the vial of water, she dripped the water on the stone. An angry hiss followed by steam rose from it. The demon in the circle cried out and moved forward. Once he reached the salt border of the circle, he slammed into an invisible wall and screamed.

"I banish you from this house, my life, and Nate's life. I banish you to your own body, to never again reach out through the Sunstone." She tossed her hand with the vial in it, splashing the water inside the circle and on the demon. His form became transparent for a brief moment then blinked in and out. For a split second, she caught a glimpse of what the demon looked like.

She repeated the incantation and the splashing of water over and over. The French doors blew open, slamming into the walls. Glass shattered and sprayed out on the floor. The wind whipped inside, blowing her hair around her face. She drew strength from the element. "Demon. Leave us!"

He roared then disappeared. The wind stopped instantly and the room felt lighter, cleaner. She dropped her shoulders, fatigue creeping in. Forcing herself to move, she rushed down to the ritual room. Relief washed through her when she opened the door and found Nate sitting up.

He let out a groan and rubbed the back of his neck. She was at his side within moments, checking him over for injuries. His gaze met hers then he framed her face and kissed her. Desire raced through her veins, along with something she swore she'd never allow herself to feel. Love.

Drawing back, she stared into his chocolate gaze. "I thought I'd lost you when I just found you. I love you."

A brilliant smile lit up his face before he pulled her in for a tight hug. "I love you, too, and I don't care that I've only known you for three days."

"Time doesn't matter when you find the one you're meant to be with. Only the heart does." Haylee's heart filled with glee. From the deepest part of her soul, she knew he was hers.

Just then, Con entered the room. "The curse on the Sunstone has been broken."

Nate squeezed her and kissed her temple. "Now what?"

Haylee frowned. Sadness darkened her mood. Nate had a job and family in California. She pulled out of his embrace and stood. "I, um, guess you will be returning to your job."

She wasn't going to cry. They could manage a long-distance relationship. Although the distance wasn't all that far.

Nate pushed to a stand and gently grabbed her arms, forcing her to face at him. "I'm staying here. I have four more days of vacation, then I'll call my dad and tell him I quit."

Happiness hummed within her. He'd give up all that for her? "Are you sure? You don't have to—"

He stopped her with a hard, passionate kiss. Breaking it too soon, he said, "I found what I'm looking for. Plus, you have inspired me to pursue my dream. I could write and help you here. That is, if you want me to stay."

"Yes, I want you to stay." She hugged him. Her heart filled with passion and a happiness she hadn't felt since she was a child. "I love you."

"I love you, too. Always."

Epilogue

Con stood next to the headstone he'd perched on a month ago, when he'd first transported to Lafayette, Oregon. It was funny how three days could change so much. Still, he wasn't sure what he was to do going forward or how the Sunstone was connected to his own curse.

His journey wasn't over. Hope started to unravel in his soul. Could he actually be free of his own prison? What would he do once he was?

The sound of leaves crunching under shoes made him turn to see Nate and Haylee walking toward him. They stopped a few feet from him and Haylee handed him the stone. "I feel I need to give this to you. I don't know why."

He took it and cupped her hand. "Thank you."

A cloaked figure appeared about a yard away. By the modest curves under the green, hooded garment, Con guessed the figure was a woman. She moved toward them, slow and careful. In her hands was a book. When she reached them, she handed Con the book. He took the leather-bound tome.

The cover had a pentagram—a five-pointed star inside a circle—and an ornate design with runes around the circle. A sun was etched in the center of the star. There were holes at each point of the star, like something had once been inlayed into the leather. On the heels of that last thought, the hooded woman took the stone from him and placed it in the top point of the star. The other holes flashed bright white for a brief moment, and then the Sunstone lit up before falling dark again. A hum of old, dark magic surrounded the book, but it only lasted a few moments.

The mystery woman took the book back and vanished. *Freedom imprisoned in elemental stones. Gather them to become flesh and bone.*

It was the same voice that had told him to find the stone. His pulse jumped. Was that the last of his curse? The part he couldn't remember? It must be. There were other cursed stones, and according the places on the book, there were four more.

Finally, he had a purpose besides being pulled from city to city. He had to find the next stone.

Turning to Nate and Haylee, he nodded. "I must go. I wish the two of you much happiness."

Haylee hugged him. "We wish for you to find your peace and happiness, as well."

The sun rose in the horizon, casting an orange and peach glow to the morning sky. Magic tingled through his body a few moments before his muscles stiffened. His back ached as wings extended from each shoulder blade. He was able to say one last good-bye before he turned to stone and everything dissolved around him. A moment later, he appeared, in gargoyle form, on the roof of a building in a city he didn't recognize.

He sighed. So he would wait for the next full moon.

The End

Coming soon in the Cursed in Stone series,
Opal's Seduction

Visit the series website for a glimpse of what is
to come: **CursedInStone.com**

Get new releases update by signing up for Lia's
newsletter: **http://eepurl.com/mBWx5**

Cursed in Stone Series

Cursed in Stone, a Gothic Romance series from Lia
Davis and Kerry Adrienne

Constantine De La Fontaine fought in the Third
Crusade, certain he was on the side of the righteous.
After being wounded in battle, he's tended to by the
beautiful and mysterious Amara, a woman who's
hiding a dangerous secret. She's the caliph's
daughter, and he's promised her hand in marriage to
the demon who's made him powerful. Con and
Amara's love is white hot, but forbidden. When the
demon finds out about their tryst, he lashes out in a
jealous rage, cursing both to live out eternity in their
own personal hells.

For centuries, Con lives as a gargoyle, cursed in stone and destined to watch others find love, with no knowledge of Amara's fate. Able to take human form only during the three nights of the full moon, he wanders the streets of the cities the curse transports him to, lost and broken hearted. Then, a whisper on the wind and a magical pull to a gemstone gives him new hope for breaking his curse and finding out what's happened to his lost love. A cloaked figure, an ancient tome, and more gemstones slowly begin to help him unravel the mystery of his curse—and possibly his freedom.

This incredible saga unfolds in a series of five novella-length stories, each set a different city around the world. The series begins with Sunstone's Fire, releasing on April 5, 2016, then followed by Opal's Seduction, Amethyst's Imbalance, Sapphire's Star, and wraps up with Emerald's Light on October 11, 2016. Learn more at: CursedInStone.com

Social Media links:

Series Website: **http://cursedinstone.com**
Facebook page: **https://www.facebook.com/Cursed-In-Stone-1567830690207365/timeline**
Publisher's website:
http://afterglowspublishing.com

About the Author

In 2008, Lia Davis ventured into the world of writing and publishing and never looked back. She has published more than twenty books, including the bestselling *A Tiger's Claim*, book one in her fan favorite Ashwood Falls series. Her novels feature compassionate yet strong alpha heroes who know how to please their women and her leading ladies are each strong in their own way. No matter what obstacle she throws at them, they come out better in the end.

While writing was initially a way escape from real world drama, Lia now makes her living creating worlds filled with magic, mystery, romance, and adventure so that *others* can leave real life behind for a few hours at a time.

Lia's favorite things are spending time with family, traveling, reading, writing, chocolate, coffee, nature and hanging out with her kitties. She and her family live in Northeast Florida battling hurricanes and very humid summers, but it's her home and she loves it!

Find out more about Lia Davis Here:

Website: **http://www.authorliadavis.com**
Newsletter: **http://eepurl.com/mBWx5**
Facebook: **https://www.facebook.com/lia.davis.52**
FB Fan Club: **www.facebook.com/liadavisfanclub/**
Twitter: @novelbylia

Other Books by Lia Davis

Paranormals

Ashwood Falls Series

Winter Eve
A Tiger's Claim
A Mating Dance
Surrendering to the Alpha
A Rebel's Heart
Divided Loyalties
Touch of Desire
A Leopard's Path
Jaguar's Judgment

Birchwood Pack

An Alpha's Fate

Bears of Blackrock
Bear Essentials
Bear Magick
A Beary Sweet Holiday

Sons of War Series

War's Passion
Ashes of War
Artemis's Hunt
Chaotic War

Shifting Magick Trilogy
Moon Curse
Moon Kissed
Moon Mated
Shifting Magick Trilogy box set

Blood and Stone (Vampire Lords)

It's A Vampire Christmas

Contemporaries

Pleasures of the Heart Series

Business Pleasures

Single Titles

His Guarded Heart